RAINA TELGEMEIER

Erinn Banting

www.av2books.com

Step 1
Go to **www.av2books.com**

Step 2
Enter this unique code
MFXKAREB9

Step 3
Explore your interactive eBook!

AV2 is optimized for use on any device

Your interactive eBook comes with...

Contents
Browse a live contents page to easily navigate through resources

Audio
Listen to sections of the book read aloud

Videos
Watch informative video clips

Weblinks
Gain additional information for research

Try This!
Complete activities and hands-on experiments

Key Words
Study vocabulary, and complete a matching word activity

Quizzes
Test your knowledge

Slideshows
View images and captions

... and much, much more!

Contents

All about Raina Telgemeier

Cartoonist Raina Telgemeier is well known for her **graphic novels**. She uses both words and drawings to tell her stories. In addition to reading the text of the books, readers can also see the characters and their reactions through the illustrations.

Raina's books are loved around the world. Some of Raina's stories are about her own life. Others come from her imagination. People can learn much from Raina's books. She often writes about topics that are difficult to talk about.

Through her graphic novels, Raina has reached millions of readers.

Raina's graphic novels have been translated into **22 languages**.

There are more than **18 million** copies of Raina's books in print.

Beginnings

Raina was born on May 26, 1977. Her parents loved the name *Reina*, a Spanish word that means "queen." On the day Raina was born, it was raining outside, so her parents changed the spelling of her name.

Raina grew up in San Francisco, California. Her father, Denis, worked as an **editor** and a writer. Her mother, Susan, was a teacher. Raina is the oldest of three children. She has a younger sister named Amara and a younger brother named Will.

Susan often read to Raina and her siblings. Raina also enjoyed reading on her own. There was a library near their house, which she liked to visit. Raina would spend hours there, reading and learning new things.

At a young age, Raina began to write and draw. She loved cartoons and animated films. When she was 9 years old, Raina started reading **comic strips**. Her father noticed how excited she was about this new hobby and took her shopping for comic books. It was here that Raina learned about other kinds of books, such as graphic novels.

Where Raina Telgemeier Was Born

OREGON
IDAHO
WYOMING
Sacramento
San Francisco
NEVADA
UTAH
Pacific Ocean
CALIFORNIA

MAP LEGEND
Capital City
City
California
United States
Mexico
Water
SCALE
0
60 Miles
60 Kilometers

San Francisco is nicknamed "The City by the Bay." The world-famous Golden Gate Bridge can be found where San Francisco Bay connects to the Pacific Ocean.

School Years

Raina's love for writing and drawing continued to grow. She began to draw cartoons as well as people that she knew. She made pictures for her middle school friends, which they displayed on the fronts of their binders. Raina's classmates called her, "the girl who could draw anything."

Raina also kept a diary. In it, she would write about important subjects, such as **anxiety**. Raina's anxiety made her scared, worried, and sick to her stomach. This was hard to discuss with others.

When she was 11 years old, Raina started adding drawings to her diary. Her diary entries became short comic strips about her life. Raina loved writing and drawing her own stories, even the difficult ones.

That same year, Raina tripped and fell, knocking out her two front teeth. The painful injury made her shy, and she was teased about the way she looked. Reading, writing, and drawing made her feel better.

When Raina first started drawing comics, she copied her favorite characters. The comic strips she liked most were *Calvin and Hobbes* and *For Better or For Worse*.

Getting Started

In high school, Raina made new friends. They were kind and supportive of Raina's talents. Raina liked to draw **caricatures** of her classmates and teachers. She even had fun with her assignments, illustrating them when she could.

Raina also used her art to help out at school. She enjoyed making posters for dances and other special events. Raina created comic strips for the school newspaper, too, which gave her a chance to share her work with other students.

After high school, Raina went to the School of Visual Arts (SVA) in New York City. There were not many female cartooning students. In Raina's cartooning class of 25 people, she was one of only two women.

While at SVA, Raina learned many new things about art. However, Raina's teachers tried to change her **style**. They criticized her drawings of faces as being too "cartoony." Nonetheless, Raina carried on. Her style worked for her, and many other people liked it as well.

Raina graduated from SVA in 2002. In total, the school has had more than 38,000 graduates. Many of them have gone on to have prestigious careers in the entertainment industry.

Early Writing

After college, Raina found a job in publishing. She liked working with people who made books, but still wanted to create stories of her own. After work each day, Raina went home and worked on her comics.

Between 2002 and 2005, Raina made seven short mini-comics, which she published herself. Each one was 12 pages long. They told the story of her life in New York City and the adventures she had with her friends.

Raina met many other artists and writers at **comic book conventions**. There, she passed out forms that advertised her work for sale. With the help of a friend, Raina made a website and started selling her mini-comics by **mail order**. Before long, she had her first fans.

In 2004, Raina met an editor who worked for a publisher called Scholastic. Raina later met with the editor's boss. When Raina told him she was a fan of a Scholastic series called The Baby-Sitters Club, it was suggested that she **adapt** a few of the books as graphic novels.

Raina sold her mini-comics for **$1.00** each.

All of Raina's graphic novels are **drawn** by **hand**.

Ann M. Martin wrote the original Baby-Sitters Club books. Raina had loved the series when she was a child.

Writing Tips

Comic strips can be an effective way to tell a story. Although it takes plenty of work to make a comic, it can also be fun. Seeing a story come alive on the page is very exciting. Raina uses different methods to help tell her stories. Young cartoonists can use these ideas as well.

Read, Read, Read

Reading is a great way to learn. Cartoonists can learn important things by reading comic strips. They can see how people tell stories. They can also observe the different ways in which people draw their characters. Raina read as many comics as she could find. This helped her to create her own style and stories.

Talk to People

Writers can learn much from talking to other people and by being good listeners. Raina paid close attention to the people she knew. She watched what they did and listened to what they said. This was very helpful since Raina's books are based on her memories of people and events.

Write Things Down

All stories start with an idea. It is important to write such ideas down. Some people use a notebook to record their ideas. Then, they can look back at their notes when they are ready to begin a story. Raina kept a diary, which she can still look at when she writes. When Raina looks at her drawings and remembers her experiences, it helps her create her books.

Road to Success

Raina started adapting her first Baby-Sitters Club book, *Kristy's Great Idea*, in 2004. Soon after, she was contacted by another editor, who worked for a website that showcased female artists. She asked Raina to share some of her work online.

Raina decided to write a new story for the website. It was about her experience of losing her front teeth. Raina began writing about this difficult time. Each week, she added the next part of the story. Readers were very interested. They kept checking the website for the next installment, to see how the story was going to progress.

By 2008, Raina was finishing her fourth Baby-Sitters Club adaptation, *Claudia and Mean Janine*. She had also written and drawn 120 pages of the story about losing her front teeth. Scholastic had been following the story online and thought it would make a great book. These comic strips later became Raina's graphic novel, *Smile*.

After Raina adapted four Baby-Sitters Club books, the series was continued by her friend and fellow cartoonist, Gale Galligan. The seventh graphic novel, *Boy-Crazy Stacey*, came out in 2019.

Smile was published by Scholastic in 2010. People enjoyed Raina's style. Many children saw themselves in her story. Adults liked *Smile* because it reminded them of experiences they had as children. By 2015, there were 1.5 million copies of *Smile* in print.

After *Smile*, Raina wrote four more books, which were all published by Scholastic. Two of them, *Sisters* and *Guts*, are about her real life. Raina also created two stories from her imagination, *Drama* and *Ghosts*.

The Publishing Process

A **manuscript** goes through many stages before it is published. Often, authors change their work to follow an editor's suggestions. The final book can look very different from what the author first wrote.

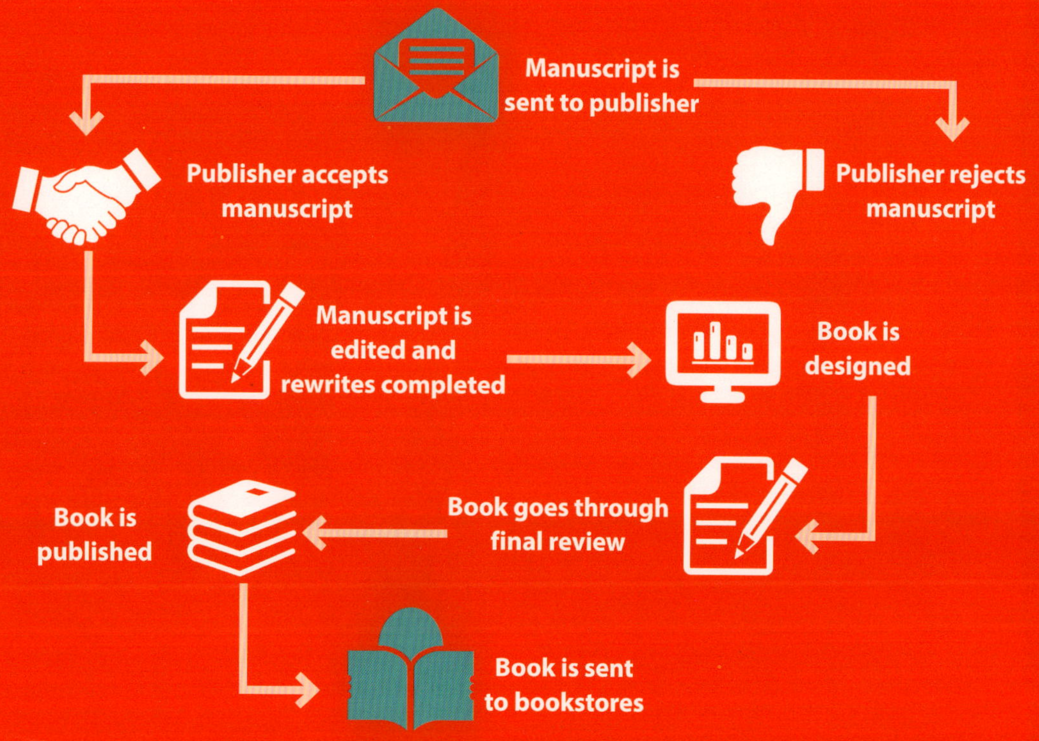

Good Reads

Raina's work has inspired many people. Her books encourage children to talk about their problems. Although she does not offer readers personal advice, Raina does want to send a positive message through her work.

Kristy's Great Idea

Raina's first Baby-Sitters Club adaptation tells Ann M. Martin's original story in graphic novel format. *Kristy's Great Idea* details the adventures of tomboy Kristy Thomas, president of the Baby-Sitters Club. She starts the club, along with her three best friends.

Meetings are held in vice-president Claudia Kishi's bedroom, where she has her own phone line. Mary Anne Spier serves as the club's secretary, and Stacey McGill acts as treasurer. The girls learn that baby-sitting might not always be easy, but no matter what happens, they will always have each other.

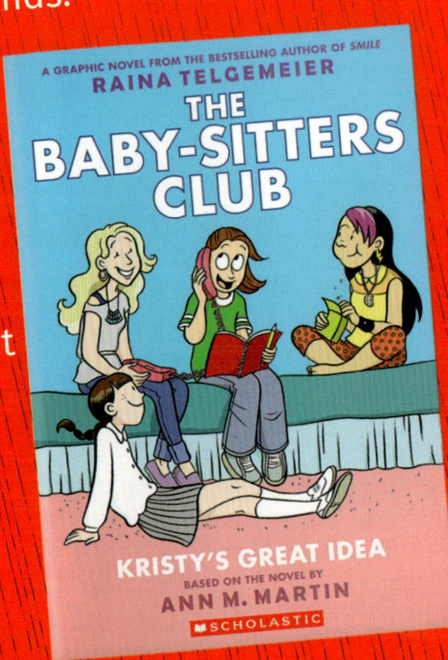

The Truth About Stacey

The Truth About Stacey is Raina's second Baby-Sitter's Club adaptation. It follows Stacey McGill, a girl who has just moved from her home in New York City to Stoneybrook, Connecticut. Not only must Stacey adapt to living in a new place, she also has to deal with finding out she has **diabetes**. Fortunately for Stacey, she has the support of her new friends and fellow Baby-Sitters Club members Kristy, Mary Anne, and Claudia, to help her face these challenges.

Smile

After Raina loses her front teeth, she finds it hard to smile about much. It takes years of treatments to get her smile back. Raina's trips to the **orthodontist** are usually painful. She thinks that surgery is scary and braces are embarrassing. She even has to wear false teeth. Growing up is hard enough without "dental drama." In this book, Raina learns several important lessons. She also goes through many big changes and dramatic events. Raina faces bullies, starts liking boys, and even lives through an earthquake.

Drama

Callie loves the theater. She is good at many things, but singing is not one of them. That is why Callie does not try out for the school play. Instead, she designs the sets for the show. Not only is this a very big job, Callie also has to deal with many complications. There is not enough money to make the set she dreams about. People in the show do not get along. The team worries that they will not sell enough tickets. When two adorable twin brothers show up, life gets really interesting.

Sisters

Raina begged her parents for a sister, but Amara is not the kind of sister she wanted. Amara is a cranky baby, then a grumpy toddler. When she is finally old enough to play with Raina, Amara does not want to play. The sisters have a hard enough time being nice to each other when they are at home. What will happen when they are stuck in a car together for a week-long road trip?

Ghosts

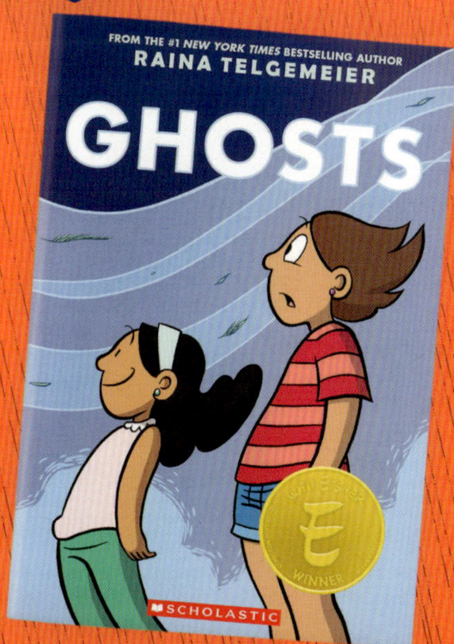

Catrina would do anything for her sister, Maya. Maya has **cystic fibrosis**, which makes it hard for her to breathe. Their family moves to a new town, in the hopes that the sea air will help Maya. There, Catrina and Maya meet Carlos. He teaches them about the ghosts that live in town. The ghosts make it hard for Maya to breathe. What will Catrina do now?

Guts

One night, Raina and her mom get really sick. They probably just have a stomach flu. The next day, things seem better, at least for Raina's mom. However, Raina notices that her tummy still bothers her, especially when she worries. This becomes a problem. Raina worries all the time. She worries about food, school, and her friends. Then, Raina starts to worry that there is something wrong with her. Raina's parents take her to the doctor. She starts talking about her problems with a special doctor called a therapist. This is when Raina finally begins to face her problems.

Milestones

Raina has always worked hard for her success. It is clear that her hard work has paid off. Today, Raina is known around the world. Readers love her graphic novels. They cannot wait to see what Raina comes up with next.

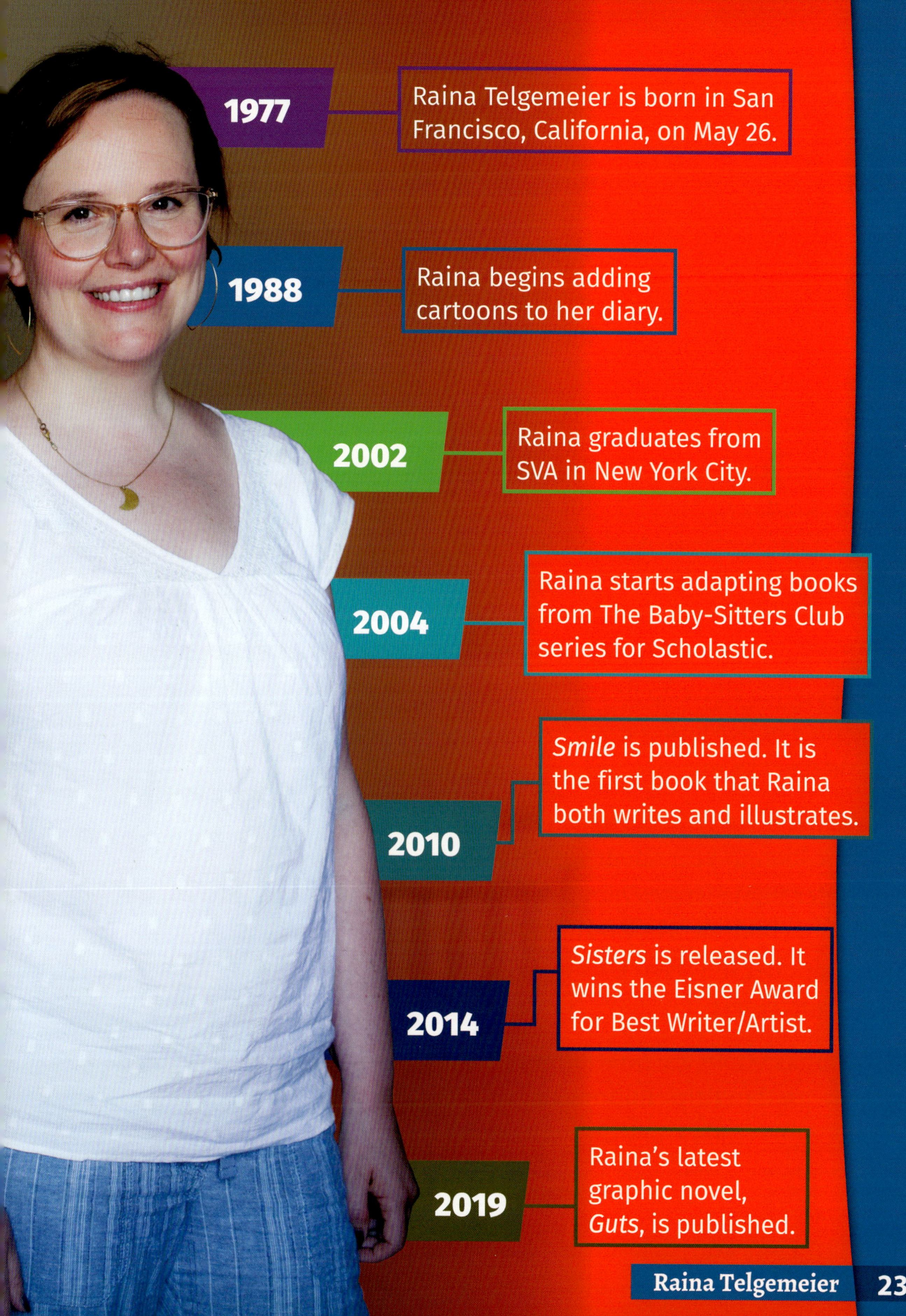

1977 Raina Telgemeier is born in San Francisco, California, on May 26.

1988 Raina begins adding cartoons to her diary.

2002 Raina graduates from SVA in New York City.

2004 Raina starts adapting books from The Baby-Sitters Club series for Scholastic.

2010 *Smile* is published. It is the first book that Raina both writes and illustrates.

2014 *Sisters* is released. It wins the Eisner Award for Best Writer/Artist.

2019 Raina's latest graphic novel, *Guts*, is published.

Telgemeier Today

Raina lives and works in San Francisco, California. People still want to read more of her work. Although Raina tries to keep up with the demand from her fans, each of her books takes years to make.

When Raina is not writing, she makes public appearances. She has spoken at several festivals and conventions. At these events, Raina talks about her life, her books, and where she gets her ideas. She also answers questions from the audience. Hundreds or even thousands of people show up to see Raina in person. Some of her talks can be found on the internet as well.

Raina often receives letters from her fans. She likes to hear about what they want to read. After Raina wrote *Drama*, she got many letters from children. They wanted to know more about her life. That is one of the reasons she wrote *Sisters*.

Raina's books are now taught in schools. They are used to help children learn to read. Her work lets kids know they are not alone, and inspires them to talk about their troubles.

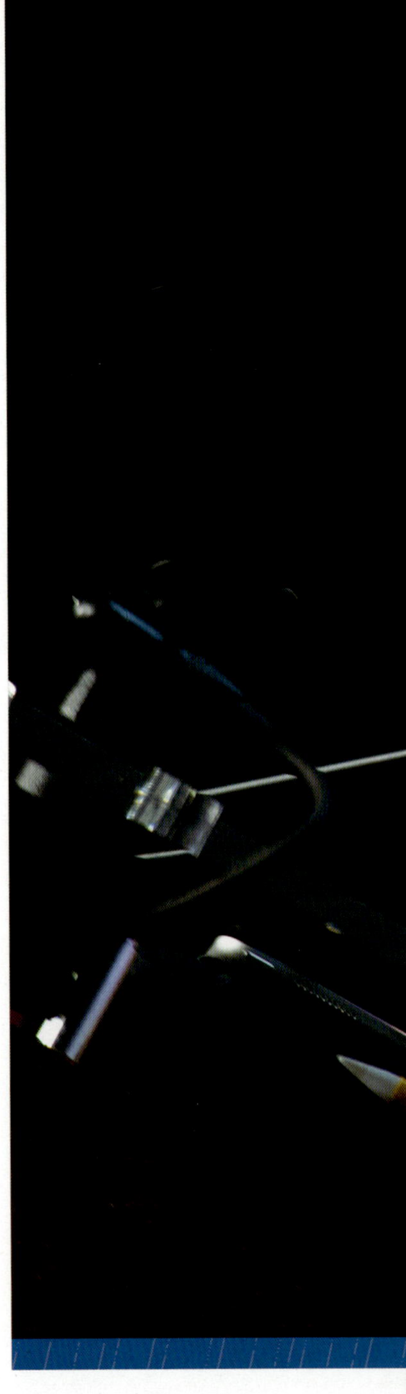

In 2019, Raina spoke at the National Book Festival in Washington, D.C.

Awards and More

Raina has received many awards for her work. In 2010, she won the Boston Globe-Horn Book Nonfiction Honor Award for *Smile*. It was the first time the prize was ever given for a graphic novel. Raina has also won three Eisner Awards. This is the top award for comic books and graphic novels. Raina won for *Smile*, *Sisters*, and *Ghosts*.

Raina's books have broken records as well. When *Guts* came out in 2019, it had a print run of 1 million copies. During the book's first week of release alone, more than 76,000 copies were sold.

In addition to her graphic novels, Raina has created other books for her fans. In 2019, she released three new books. *Share Your Smile: Raina's Guide to Telling Your Own Story* includes tips for children who want to write and illustrate stories of their own. Each page of *Raina's Mini Posters: 20 Prints to Decorate Your Space at Home and at School* features a page from one of Raina's graphic novels. Raina also put out an illustrated journal with prompts for children, called *My Smile Diary*.

Raina's next book is tentatively scheduled to be released in 2021.

All of Raina's books have been on the *New York Times* Best Sellers list. This list tracks the highest-selling books in the United States.

Writing a Biography

All of the parts of a biography work together to tell the story of a person's life. Find out how these elements combine by writing a biography. Begin by choosing a person whose story fascinates you. You will have to research the person's life by using library books and reliable websites. You can also email the person or write him or her a letter. The person might agree to answer your questions directly.

Parts of a Biography

Early Life

- Where and when was the person born?
- What is known about the person's family and friends?
- Did the person grow up in unusual circumstances?

Growing Up

- Who had the most influence on the person?
- Did he or she receive assistance from others?
- Did the person have a positive attitude?

Developing Skills

- What was the person's education?
- What was the person's first job or work experience?
- What obstacles did the person overcome?

Early Achievements

- What was the person's most important early success?
- What processes did this person use in his or her work?
- Which of the person's traits were most helpful in his or her work?

Person Today

- Has the person received awards or recognition for accomplishments?
- What is the person's life's work?
- How have the person's accomplishments served others?

Quiz

1 Where and when was Raina born?

2 Into how many languages have Raina's books been translated?

3 What is Raina's sister's name?

4 What difficult subject did Raina write about in her diary?

5 Where did Raina go to college?

6 How many mini-comics did Raina make after college?

7 What is the name of the first book Raina both wrote and illustrated?

8 How many Eisner Awards has Raina won?

ANSWERS

1. Raina was born on May 26, 1977, in San Francisco, California. **2.** 22 **3.** Amara **4.** Her anxiety **5.** The School of Visual Arts (SVA) **6.** Seven **7.** *Smile* **8.** Three

Author Speak

The field of writing has its own language. Understanding some of the more common writing terms will allow you to discuss your ideas about books.

action: the moving events of a work of fiction

antagonist: the person in a story who opposes the main character

autobiography: a history of a person's life written by that person

biography: a written account of another person's life

character: a person in a story, poem, or play

climax: the most exciting moment or turning point in a story

episode: a scene or short piece of action in a story

fiction: stories about characters and events that are not real

foreshadow: to hint at something that is going to happen later in a story

imagery: a written description of a thing or idea that brings an image to mind

narrator: the speaker of a story who relates its events

nonfiction: writing that deals with real people and events

novel: published writing of considerable length that portrays characters within a story

plot: the order of events in a work of fiction

protagonist: the leading character of a story; often a likable character

resolution: the end of a story, when the conflict is settled

scene: a single episode in a story

setting: the place and time in which a work of fiction occurs

theme: an idea that runs throughout a work of fiction

Key Words

adapt: to modify for a new use

anxiety: feeling nervous, worried, or fearful

caricatures: drawings with distortions or extreme exaggerations of particular features

cartoonist: a person who does simple, exaggerated drawings, usually of a humorous subject

comic book conventions: events with a primary focus on comic books and comic book culture, where fans gather to meet creators, experts, and each other

comic strips: stories written in short form, with drawings

cystic fibrosis: a progressive disease that causes lung infections and makes breathing difficult

diabetes: a disease that impairs the body's production of a hormone called insulin, making it difficult to maintain healthy blood sugar levels

editor: someone who prepares a manuscript for publication

graphic novels: novels in comic strip format that are published as books

mail order: a method of selling goods remotely, and then delivering them to customers by mail

manuscript: a draft of a story before it is published

orthodontist: a dentist who treats irregularities in the jaws or teeth

style: a particular manner or technique by which something is done, created, or performed

Index

Get the best of both worlds.

AV2 bridges the gap between print and digital.

The expandable resources toolbar enables quick access to content including **videos**, **audio**, **activities**, **weblinks**, **slideshows**, **quizzes**, and **key words**.

Animated videos make static images come alive.

Resource icons on each page help readers to further **explore key concepts**.

Published by AV2
14 Penn Plaza 9th Floor
New York, NY 10122
Website: www.av2books.com

Library of Congress Control Number: 2020939591

ISBN 978-1-7911-3178-4 (hardcover)
ISBN 978-1-7911-3179-1 (softcover)
ISBN 978-1-7911-3180-7 (multi-user eBook)
ISBN 978-1-7911-3181-4 (single-user eBook)

Printed in Guangzhou, China
1 2 3 4 5 6 7 8 9 0 24 23 22 21 20

072020
101319

Editor: Katie Gillespie
Designer: Ana María Vidal

AV2 acknowledges Getty Images, Alamy, Newscom, Dreamstime, Shutterstock, and Wikimedia Commons as its primary image suppliers for this title.